ROBO-RUNNERS

Aquanauts

www.damianharvey.co.uk

Books in the **Robo-Runners** series:

ROBO-RUNNERS

Aquanauts

by DAMIAN HARVEY

Illustrated by Mark Oliver

h
Hodder
Children's
Books

A division of Hachette Children's Books

For Rachel Harvey
with lots of love

The ancient city of Tarka stood between the desert dunes of the Ghost Sea and the North Polar Wastelands.

A great wall had been built to hold back the once-great sea and reclaim land for the ever-growing city. Houses, towers and palaces had risen up between flowing waterways, and a network of bridges and high walkways had joined them together.

The city had been rich and powerful – but that was many years ago. The world had moved on and the people had left after the Ghost Sea dried up, leaving the city to fall into ruin.

Towards this ancient city came four robot friends, Crank, Al, Grunt and Avatar, travelling in search of a safe place for old robots.

A place where robots can be free to live their lives in peace.

A place called Robotika.

It had taken longer than they'd expected to reach the city walls and the sun was starting to rise as they began to climb the huge stone steps.

"These must have been built for giants," complained Crank, sitting down to rest. "If I take one more step I think my joints will fall apart."

"The steps weren't built for people to climb at all," said Avatar as she clambered up next to Crank. "They were built to protect the city against the sea."

Al hovered down to see what the two friends were up to. "There is no time to rest," he said. "You *said* we should get over the wall before the sun comes up."

"He's right," said Avatar, helping Crank to his feet. "We should be safe once we get over this wall and away from the Ghost Sea."

"It's all right for him," grumbled Crank. "He doesn't have to walk."

Since having his legs pulled off in the recycling plant, Al had been forced to walk around on his hands – until Avatar had given him an anti-gravity belt. Now, Al hovered whenever he could.

"I think you should walk too," said Avatar, examining Al's belt. "These power cells are getting very low."

"I am sure they will be fine," said Al. "And they will soon recharge when the sun comes up."

As Al flew off up the steps, Crank shook his head. "He never listens, you know. He'll end up having to walk with the rest of us and *then* he'll start complaining."

"Never mind," said Avatar. "We can all have a rest when we get into the city."

"I can hardly wait," said Crank. "Tarka sounds like a wonderful place."

"It is," said Avatar. "Once the humans had left, it became a city run *by* robots *for* robots."

"It sounds almost as good as Robotika," said Crank.

Behind them, Grunt was lumbering up the stone steps, slowly but surely, with Scamp, the robo-dog, by his side. "I fink we is nearly at da top, Scamp," said Grunt, pulling himself up with one huge hand.

The big botweiler kept stopping to look down across the Ghost Sea that stretched out behind them. Baring his razor-sharp teeth, Scamp let out a deep growl.

"I know," said Grunt, patting Scamp's head. "Dare is somefink followin' us … but don't you worry. Old Grunt is keeping his eyes open."

Just before the four friends reached the top of the wall, Avatar stopped them. "I think *I'd* better go first," she said. "The guards might not be happy to see strangers climbing over the wall."

"*Guards!*" cried Crank. "I thought you said this was a *peaceful* city and that we'd be welcome here."

"It is peaceful," said Avatar. "But all cities have enemies – even an ancient city like Tarka."

"But what makes you think they'll recognise you?" asked Crank.

Avatar stopped and looked down at the three friends. "They will recognise me because I used to be part of their defence force," she said. "Now wait here."

The three friends looked at each other in amazement as Avatar climbed on to the top of the wall and disappeared from view.

"*Part of their defence force?*" said Crank, shrugging his shoulders. "I didn't even know she'd *been* to Tarka before."

"She said she was a powerball player," said Grunt.

"There seems to be a lot about Avatar that we do not know," said Al. "But I feel sure we will be learning more about her very soon."

The three friends waited for what seemed like a long time, but Avatar didn't return.

"I fink somefink must be wrong," said Grunt. "Someone should take a look."

Al adjusted the dial on his anti-grav belt and rose slowly into the air towards the top of the wall. From where they stood, Crank and Grunt could see their friend peering over the top.

"Well!" said Crank. "Can you see Avatar?"

"Yes," said Al, coming back down to join them. "But it is very strange."

"Strange!" said Crank. "What's strange? Is she in trouble?"

"I do not think so," said Al. "She is just standing there."

"Come on," said Grunt. "Let's take a look."

The big robot jumped and grabbed the top of the wall with one hand then pulled himself up. Scamp, the botweiler, leaped up to join him and Crank followed closely behind.

"I do hope Avatar does not mind us coming up to join her," said Al. "After all, she did tell us to wait."

The three
robots joined their
friend on top of the wall as the morning sun
shed its light over the ancient city.

A few tall towers and buildings reached up,
almost level with the top of the wall. Other
than that, all they could see were the rooftops,
platforms and bridges that rose above the surface
of what looked like a giant lake. Green murky
water lapped against the walls and slimy weed
clung to the ancient stones.

"Oh!" said Al. "It is not quite what I had expected."

Avatar turned her head slowly and looked at him.

"It's gone," she said. "The city has gone."

"Gone?" said Crank. "What do you mean, it's gone?"

"This water shouldn't be here," said Avatar. "These walls were built to keep the water out, not keep it in."

"But where are the robots?" asked Crank. "Where are the guards?"

"Look!" said Al, pointing. "There is someone over there."

Looking across the water towards one of the towers, the three friends were just in time to see a figure disappearing into the darkness within.

"That didn't look like a robot," said Crank.

"Perhaps it was one of dem softies," said Grunt.

"No," said Avatar, shaking her head. "I don't think it was a human but I have a horrible feeling I know what it was … I can only hope that I'm wrong."

2

"If it wasn't a robot or a softie, then what was it?" asked Crank.

"It looked like one of the Crodilus," said Avatar, "but I don't know what it's doing here. They normally live in the Swamplands."

"Are they dangerous?" asked Al.

"Oh yes," said Avatar. "The Crodilus are nasty, aggressive creatures and they are obsessed with technology. They used to sneak into the city and steal anything they could get their hands on – generators, engine pods, weapons and anything else that was lying around."

"Well," said Al, "I think we should leave before more of them come."

"We can't go back to the Ghost Sea," said Crank, looking worried. "We might bump into Gore and his robot pirates."

"And I never wants to see doze giant crabs again," said Grunt, scowling.

The three friends looked at Grunt's arm and Crank shuddered at the thought of the giant crab that had bitten the big robot's hand off with the snip of one deadly pincer.

"No!" agreed Al, shaking his head. "We can not go back there."

"You're right," said Avatar. "The only way is to go forwards, across to the other side of the city."

"How are we gonna get across dere?" asked Grunt. "Grunt can't swim."

"Perhaps I could carry you across," suggested Al.

"I really don't think that's a good idea," said Avatar. "Anti-grav belts are only made to support one robot at a time."

"You may have forgotten," said Al, "but I am the very latest in robot technology. I am constructed from ultra-lightweight, hard-wearing materials and am much lighter than older models. I am sure the anti-grav belt could carry me and another robot without much difficulty."

Despite a few bumps and scratches, and having his legs pulled off by the Tin Man in the recycling plant, Al was still quite a new robot and never missed a chance to remind his friends just how up to date he was.

"You might be right," said Avatar. "But you

should wait for the belt's power cells to recharge before trying anything like that. For now we can go across that walkway."

Al reluctantly agreed and switched off the anti-grav belt. Walking on his hands, he followed the others along the wall to a narrow stone walkway that stretched over the water towards the top of one of the towers.

"It doesn't *look* very strong," said Crank, looking down at the water. "Are you sure it's safe?"

"Of course it is," said Al. "This walkway has probably been here for hundreds of years, so it is *even* older than you are. I am sure it can take our weight. Of course I *could* always hover across if that would help."

"No!" said Avatar. "We'll walk, but Crank is right, it might not be as safe as it looks so it might be best if we go one at a time."

"*Not as safe as it looks!*" said Crank. "I don't think it looks safe at all."

"Don't worry," said Avatar, stepping on to the walkway. "I'll go first."

The three friends watched as Avatar easily crossed the narrow walkway and reached the tower at the other side.

As soon as she was across, Grunt set off with Scamp, the robo-dog, right behind him.

"Oh great," moaned Crank. "Grunt's so big he'll probably loosen all the stones and it'll collapse as soon as I set foot on it."

"Of course," said Al, "if you are frightened, you could always wait here."

"Frightened!" said Crank. "I'm not frightened of anything." And with that, he stepped on to the walkway and started striding across. But as he went, Crank's steps got slower and slower until he'd almost come to a complete stop.

"I can't go any further," said Crank nervously. "The stones keep moving. I can hear them rattling and groaning beneath my feet."

"You'll be fine," said Avatar, encouragingly. "Just keep going. You're almost across."

"*I can't do it!*" cried Crank, dropping on to his hands and knees. "*Just leave me here to rust.*"

"Hey!" said Grunt. "I can hear da stones moving too."

The four friends listened carefully and they all heard it. A faint rattling sound that was gradually getting louder – but it wasn't coming from the stone walkway.

"Something's coming," said Avatar. "Quick! Into the tower."

"YOU CAN'T JUST LEAVE ME HERE!" yelled Crank.

"Well, get moving," said Al, running across the walkway behind him.

"Don't you tell me to get moving, you bucket head," snapped Crank as he got shakily to his feet.

"Well, *I* cannot get past until *you* get out of the way, you bag of bolts," said Al.

As the two friends stood and argued in the middle of the walkway, the rattling sound grew louder and something swooped down towards them from above one of the towers.

"DUCK!" cried Avatar.

Crank felt himself being shoved to the floor as a large shape whizzed overhead.

"What was that?" asked Al.

"A Dragonfly," said Avatar. "And one of the Crodilus is flying it. Now come on, before it comes back."

Avatar grabbed Crank's hand and dragged him to his feet, pulling him across the walkway towards the tower at the other side.

"Quickly!" she said. "It's coming."

As she spoke, the huge Dragonfly came back, rattling and buzzing through the air towards them, its plasma cannon spitting out balls of green fire that shot past their heads and fizzed into the water.

One of the fireballs hit the walkway, making the stones shudder beneath Al's hands. He stumbled and fell flat on his face.

Avatar and Crank had just reached the safety of the tower when the Dragonfly buzzed past them again. As it rattled through the air, Crank could see the Crodilus pilot glaring at them from its seat, its lips pulled back in a hideous grin exposing a long row of teeth.

"That horrible creature is enjoying this," said Crank.

"I said they were nasty," said Avatar. "And they *hate* robots."

"*They hate robots!*" cried Crank. "You didn't mention *that* before."

"I didn't want to worry you," said Avatar.

"I'll sort dat Dragonfly out," said Grunt, stepping back on to the walkway with a huge stone in his hand.

Al had got up but didn't know which way to run as the Dragonfly came in again with its plasma cannon blazing. Another hail of green fireballs hit the stones and exploded around him.

Grunt pulled his arm back and threw the huge stone as hard as he could.

The stone shot through the air, straight towards the Dragonfly, but the pilot had already seen what was happening and easily dropped beneath it.

As the huge stone splashed harmlessly into the water, the Crodilus pulled at the controls of the Dragonfly, twisting and turning through the air to get Al back in its sights. The Dragonfly's wings squealed and groaned under the strain and the Crodilus roared with rage and fired at Al once again.

Al felt the walkway shake beneath him as another ball of fire hit it, then there was a loud whine from the Dragonfly behind him.

From where they stood, Avatar, Crank and Grunt saw the Dragonfly's wings hit the surface of the water, making it twist to one side, and they watched as the Crodilus tried desperately to keep the flying machine under control. But it was no use.

The Dragonfly flipped over and crashed into the walkway. The columns that supported it toppled into each other like dominoes and collapsed, crushing the Dragonfly and dragging it down beneath the water with them.

Al was running as fast as he could but the walkway was collapsing beneath him and there was nothing Crank, Avatar or Grunt could do apart from watch as their friend dropped into the murky water below.

3

The three robots watched as ripples chased each other across the surface of the water. They lapped against the towers and walls, but after a while, even they died away. Soon there was nothing left to show that anything had happened at all.

"I can't believe he's gone," said Crank. "It's all my fault."

"Yeah, it is," said Grunt, sadly.

"No," said Avatar, "it's my fault. If I'd let him use the anti-grav belt he'd never have fallen."

"Dat's right too," said Grunt. "An' if I'd hit dat Dragonfly it would never have crashed into the walkway."

"Perhaps he's all right," said Crank hopefully. "He *was* a new robot, after all. The very latest in robot technology."

"But those stone blocks are very heavy," said Avatar, shaking her head.

"Yeah, an' dat water looks very wet," said Grunt. "An' robots an' water does not go together."

"You're right," said Crank, looking down into the murky water. "Al's gone …"

"Come on," said Avatar. "We should go too. There might be more of the Crodilus hanging round and I'm sure Al would have wanted us to carry on."

Crank nodded his head and followed Avatar, Grunt and Scamp into the tower behind them. Avatar was right, Al would have wanted them to carry on and find Robotika – even if he wasn't with them – but it just wouldn't be the same without him.

The tower was damp and gloomy inside.

A stone staircase spiralled up against one wall and another led down into the darkness below. Wires ran along the wall to empty power sockets and light fittings, but anything of any use had been taken out long ago.

Set against the far wall was a heavy wooden door, but that was locked and the control panel next to it had been smashed.

"There's nothing up there," said Avatar, coming back down from the roof. "Apart from a view of the city."

"An' dese stairs just go down into da water," said Grunt. "Da rest of da tower's flooded."

"We'll have to go through that door," said Avatar.

"Do you think you could open it for us?"

"Of course," said Grunt. "I is an expert wiv doors."

The big robot lumbered across to the door, stood up straight, then knocked on it gently with the knuckles of one huge hand.

"Allo!" called Grunt. "Is dere anybody dere?"

"What *are* you doing?" asked Crank.

"I is being polite," said Grunt. "You should *always* knock first."

Then the huge robot gave the door a gentle shove.

There was a loud bang as the heavy door flew back off its hinges and crashed to the floor. The wooden doorframe splintered and dust trickled down from the stones above it.

"Thank you, Grunt," said Avatar, stepping across the broken doorway and back outside.

"It was my pleasure," said Grunt, following her through.

Crank shook his head as he followed his two friends through the doorway and out on to the walkway beyond it.

This second walkway was wider than the one they had crossed at the other side of the tower and had a low wall running along each side of it. The only problem was, this walkway sloped down towards the water.

"Now where do we go?" asked Crank.

"If we can get on to that block we should be able to make it to the landing platform over there," said Avatar.

Crank looked across to the landing platform that stood just above the surface of the water. Strands of green weed hung down from its edges like a beard and the rusted remains of a vehicle stood in the middle of it. Puddles of green water had gathered on the platform and storage crates and other bits of junk lay scattered across it.

Between the walkway and the landing pad was a row of large stone blocks that poked above the surface of the water like giant stepping stones.

"We'll *never* make it across there," said Crank.

"Of course we will," said Avatar. "I've done it loads of times."

"What do you mean, you've done it loads of times?" asked Crank.

"Those blocks are on the roof of the hangar," said Avatar. "It's where we kept the Dragonflies and other craft. Jumping across the blocks was the quickest way of getting from the roof to the landing platform – I used to do it all the time."

As Avatar headed off down the sloping walkway, Crank and Grunt looked at each other and shrugged.

"I don't know what she's on about," said Grunt, shaking his head.

As they reached the bottom of the sloping walkway, Avatar took two quick steps then

somersaulted through the air and landed gracefully
on the first of the
large stone
blocks.

"Wow!" said
Crank. "She's amazing, isn't she?"

"Yeah well," said Grunt. "I could do dat if I
wanted to."

The big robot lumbered down the walkway and leaped across the gap, grabbing hold of the block with his hand and easily pulling himself up.

"Dare you are," said Grunt, nodding his head. "Your turn."

"Come on!" said Avatar encouragingly. "It's easy."

Crank looked at the stretch of water that lay between the walkway and the stone block where his friends were now standing. It looked a long way to jump and the block was quite high. He'd need a good run-up.

After taking a few steps back, Crank charged down the slope and leaped across the gap.

"Yaaaaa!" he cried as he flew through the air. Then—

CRASH!

Crank smashed into the side of the stone block and hung there for a moment, gripping the top with his hands.

"Are you all right?" said Avatar, looking down at Crank.

"Oh yes," he groaned. "I'll be fine. Just having a little rest before I pull myself up."

When Crank didn't move, Grunt reached down and grabbed him with one huge hand. "Up you get," he said, lifting Crank into the air and putting him down on the stone block.

"When you're ready," said Avatar, "we'll carry on to the landing pad. The rest of the blocks are quite close together so it should be easy."

"Don't you worry about me," said Crank. "I've jumped across much bigger gaps than this before ... I'll see you on the landing pad."

And before Avatar or Grunt could say anything, Crank had gone and was leaping across the water from stone to stone.

"Come on," said Avatar. "We'd better keep up with him."

Grunt and Scamp charged across the stepping stones side by side, right behind Avatar, and they caught up with Crank just before he reached the landing platform.

"What's the matter?" asked Avatar. "Why have you stopped?"

Crank was standing at the very edge of the last stone, looking at the water. "You'd better come and see," he said. "There something down here."

It had obviously been there for a very long time – hanging part in and part out of the water. Thick chains were fastened to its wrists and the other ends were secured to metal rings on the edge of the landing platform.

The robot looked as though it was made of nothing but rust, and flakes of it were falling off into the water that lapped against its chest. Green weeds had wrapped themselves around one of the robot's arms and its head hung down loosely on its neck.

"Who would do this?" asked Crank.

"The Crodilus," said Avatar. "I said they hated

robots. Come on, let's see if we can lift it out of the water. No robot deserves to be left like this."

The three friends jumped across to the landing platform and, taking hold of the chains, they carefully started to lift the robot's body out of the murky water. The robot was almost out when its head jerked round and one of its eyes flickered brightly for a moment.

"RUN!" screamed the robot. "THEY ARE COMING FOR US A—"

Then with a crunch, the robot collapsed in a shower of rust and dropped into the water beneath them.

Crank and Avatar were left holding the lengths of chain that had been fastened to the robot's wrists. They looked down into the water at the side of the landing platform but all that could be seen were the remains of one arm, tangled in the weeds, and a few bubbles as they rose to the surface.

"Dare was nuffink you could do," said Grunt, shaking his head. "When a robot looks like dat dare is nuffink anyone can do."

"I know," said Crank, still watching the bubbles. "It just surprised me when it shouted out like that. I wonder what it meant?"

"It's probably nuffink," said Grunt. "I used to see old robots do that back in the junk yard. It's just a tiny bit of energy left in the circuits and when you move dem dey suddenly makes a noise."

"But what was it doing chained to this landing platform?" asked Crank.

"The Crodilus probably put it there as a warning

to keep other robots away," said Avatar.

"Well it works for me," said Crank, still watching the bubbles. "I think we should go away as soon as we can."

Avatar agreed with him but before she could say anything Scamp let out a loud metallic growl.

"What is it, boy?" asked Grunt, going over to see what the botweiler had found.

The big robo-dog had wandered across to the far side of the landing platform and was looking over the edge into the water.

"It's just more of dem bubbles," said Grunt. "There's lots of dem here."

"There's lots of them over here too," said Avatar, walking round the outside of the platform and peering down into the water.

"I've got a bad feeling about this," said Crank, moving away from the edge.

"You're right," growled Grunt. "I fink we should get out of 'ere right now."

The three friends
started to walk across the platform
but stopped suddenly as the water erupted in front
of them and something started to rise out of it.

"This way," shouted Avatar, changing direction
then stopping again as another shape erupted from
the water.

"It's no use," said Crank. "They're all around us."

Scamp bared his razor-sharp teeth and growled
at the shapes as they broke through the surface of

the water. Crank, Avatar and Grunt slowly backed
towards the middle of the platform, but there was
nowhere to hide. They were completely surrounded.

Six enormous figures rose from the water and
stepped on to the platform around the three robot
friends. They towered over Crank and even made
Grunt look small.

Five of the figures held enormous energy
weapons that steamed and clicked as they took up
positions around the platform, their feet thudding
heavily as they moved. The figures kept their
weapons raised and slowly turned their heads,
scanning the air as if looking for something.

The sixth figure looked slightly different from the others. There were lightning stripes across its chest and it was carrying some kind of box. As the others kept guard it walked slowly towards the three friends.

"What *are* they?" asked Crank, trying to keep as far away from the figures as he could.

"I've no idea," said Avatar. "I've never seen anything like them before."

"Dey is Aquanauts," said Grunt, nodding his head knowingly.

"How do you know that?" asked Avatar.

"It sez so on dare suits," said Grunt. "Look – Aquanaut 3000."

"Oh yes," said Avatar, noticing the writing on the Aquanaut's shoulder.

"What do you think they want?" asked Crank.

"I doesn't know," growled Grunt. "But I isn't going to stand here while dey dangle us in da water like dat other poor robot."

Grunt wrapped the length of chain he was holding round his hand and started swinging it above his head. "Come on den," he roared. "Let's see if you like da feel of dis."

The Aquanaut with the lightning stripes and the box suddenly stopped and the others quickly turned to face Grunt.

Five red targeting lasers danced over Grunt's body and the air was filled with a high-pitched humming sound as five energy guns powered up.

"Nwod ti tup," said one of the Aquanauts, its voice sounding dull and lifeless.

"What did it say?" asked Grunt.

"I'm not sure," replied Avatar, "but I think it wants you to put the chain down."

"Nwod ti tup," repeated the Aquanaut, pointing at the floor.

Scamp let out a whine and Grunt nodded his head. "I fink you is right," he said, dropping the chain on to the platform. "I suppose we'd better do what dey wants."

The energy guns clicked and hissed again as they powered down and the Aquanaut with the lightning stripes and the box stepped forwards and laid it on the platform at Avatar's feet.

"Llits dnats," said the Aquanaut, stepping away from them.

"I think it wants us to stand still," said Avatar.

"How do you know that?" asked Crank.

But Avatar didn't get a chance to answer. The box on the floor bleeped three times and pool of bright blue gel seeped out from it and poured across the floor.

The gel fizzed and crackled as it crept beneath the robots' feet before rising into the air to form a giant sphere around them.

Crank reached out and gently touched the inside of the sphere with one hand. Then he knocked on it with his knuckles.

"It's set as hard as stone," he said.

"I fink we is trapped," said Grunt.

5

From inside the sphere everything on the outside looked blue and foggy, but Crank could just make out the shape of one of the Aquanauts as it walked towards them.

"Now what's it trying to say?" asked Crank.

"I'm not quite sure," said Avatar, looking at the Aquanaut as it waved its arms around in the air.

As they watched, the Aquanaut put its hands on the outside of the sphere and slowly pushed them forwards. Crank and the others staggered around inside as the whole thing started to roll across the landing platform.

It was difficult at first, but once they'd got their

balance, the three friends found it quite easy to walk along inside the sphere and were just getting used to it when they reached the edge of the platform.

"I fink we is going in da water," said Grunt.

There was a dull splash when the sphere hit the water and the three friends fell over each other. Scamp let out a growl.

The Aquanauts had dropped into the water around them, and with a series of muffled noises – *THUB, THUB, THUB* – handles were attached to the side of the blue sphere.

With each of them gripping a handle, the Aquanauts slowly sank into the water, taking the three friends down with them.

"Wow!" said Crank. "This looks amazing."

Crank was on his hands and knees peering through the bottom of the sphere. Once they'd gone a little way beneath the surface, the pale blue of the sphere seemed to become almost perfectly clear and the water no longer appeared green and murky.

The whole of the flooded city came into view and Crank could see huge shoals of fish swimming between the pillars and sunken bridges. Giant eels snaked through darkened windows and a massive stingray was gliding gracefully above one of the old walkways.

The once-great city of Tarka had become home to all sorts of wildlife,

but not all of the buildings and walkways had been abandoned to the sea.

Pale lights shone from the windows of more than a dozen buildings, and thick tubes, made from the same material as the sphere, snaked between the ruins and joined these buildings together.

The three friends watched as the Aquanauts dragged them down into the depths of the water and through the open roof of one of the smaller buildings. As they passed through it, the roof closed above their heads and the sphere they were riding in came to rest on the floor.

A loud humming sound came from outside the sphere and through its surface Crank could see the water level in the room steadily creeping down. Once out of the water, the wall of the sphere gradually returned to its pale blue colour and everything outside went foggy again.

Through it all, Crank could just make out the shape of one of the Aquanauts as it aimed its energy gun at them, and fired.

Crank let out a loud scream as the energy gun flashed, but it was instantly drowned out by the sound of the sphere exploding, Scamp howling, and something soft and sticky splattering on to his face and body.

When the noise in the room had died away, Crank opened his eyes. He was relieved to find he was still in one piece, though they were all covered in great globs of sticky blue gel that could only be the remains of the sphere.

Wiping the gel from his face, Crank saw the room they were standing in was small and square. There was a heavy metal door set in one of the walls and a row of pods stood against the others like glass sarcophagi.

"Auqa ot emoclew," said one of the Aquanauts.

"What?" said Grunt.

"I think it said welcome to Aqua," said Avatar.

"Why doesn't dey talk properly den," said Grunt.

"They appear to be talking backwards," explained Avatar.

While she was speaking, the six Aquanauts moved towards the outside of the room and each of them stepped backwards into the empty pods that were standing there.

Crank watched as the Aquanauts fell back into the pods and one by one started to make a hissing noise. With a loud CRACK that sounded like an egg bursting open, the Aquanauts began to split in half, letting out jets of steam from all their joints.

"What are they doing?" said Crank.

But Avatar and Grunt didn't answer – they were too busy staring at the Aquanauts.

As the steam cleared, Crank could see that every joint on the Aquanauts' bodies had grown wider, letting them see inside, beyond the heavy armour.

"There's something in there," said Crank.

"An' I fink it's comin' out," said Grunt.

A tall thin robot stepped out of one of the pods, leaving the open Aquanaut 3000 suit behind it.

"Sorry about the confusion," said the robot. "The vocal relays on the 3000s are still transposing dialogue."

"What?" said Grunt, with a frown.

"He said the suits make it sound like they're talking backwards," explained Avatar.

"Why didn't he just say dat den," said Grunt, shaking his head.

"Oh …" said Crank, finally understanding what was going on. "Those things are just suits."

"Not *just* suits," snapped the robot. "The Aquanaut 3000 is an all-purpose power suit. It is designed to provide full support and give ultimate protection and manoeuvrability to *any* robot in *any* environment. They can be used in extreme cold and unbearable heat. They can be used beneath the water and even in outer space."

"*And* dey makes you talk backwards," said
Grunt, nodding with approval.

"Yes," agreed the robot, reluctantly, "but that is
just a minor problem and I am sure I will get that
sorted out before too long."

"I fink dey is pretty cool," said Grunt.

"Oh," said the robot, cheering up a little. "That
is very kind of you. I am very proud of the
Aquanaut 3000. They are my greatest invention."

"Then you must be Archimender," said Avatar.
"You invented the Dragonflies and the—"

"Yes, yes, yes," interrupted the robot. "I am
Archimender. You, my dear, are Avatar, one of the
defenders of Tarka – although we never met I
heard all about you – but alas, Tarka is no more.
This is Aqua."

"But what happened?" asked Avatar.

"The Crodilus happened," said Archimender.
"Shortly after you left, they destroyed the
northern gate and the floodwaters broke through.

Within a few hours, most of the city was under water. Hundreds of robots were destroyed."

"I should have been here," said Avatar, sadly. "I could have helped them."

"You would have been destroyed too," said Archimender. "The defence force were at the gate when it was blown apart. I am sorry ... but not one of them survived."

Avatar bowed her head sadly. "I should still have been here," she said. "They were my friends."

"Oh!" cried Archimender. "I almost forgot. One of your friends is here. We found him in the water – just before we found you."

Crank, Avatar and Grunt looked at each other ...

"Al!" they cried together.

6

Archimender led the three friends through one
of the tubes that joined different parts of the
underwater city together. Through its pale blue
wall, Crank could see bright yellow fish darting
this way and that through the ruins of one of the
other buildings. Everything seemed so peaceful
beneath the water.

"We knew the Crodilus were planning to
flood the city," said Archimender, tapping on the
side of the tube as they walked along, "so we
started to seal the buildings in this aqua-shell.
We thought there was plenty of time ... but we
were wrong."

"Why didn't you just leave the city and find somewhere else to live?" asked Crank.

"Where would we go?" asked Archimender. "This city is all we know. The world outside is not always a safe place for robots and not everyone is brave enough to leave like Avatar did."

"I still don't understand how it happened," said Avatar. "The Crodilus were always causing trouble but they were very primitive. They never had the technology to do any *real* damage."

"We were betrayed," said Archimender. "Someone let the Crodilus into the city. They stole Dragonflies and weapons. They destroyed the computers and sabotaged our security systems."

"But *who* would do that?" asked Crank.

"Gore!" said Avatar, nodding her head.

"Gore?" cried Crank, his eyes opening wide. "Not the same Gore that was leading the robot pirates?"

"Yes," said Avatar. "The same one. That's how we knew each other. Gore came down to the city from the North Polar Spaceport. He was nice at first and seemed very keen to settle in Tarka — after all, it was a place where robots could be free. I even got him to join the defence force as he seemed perfect for the job and was excellent with all kinds of weapons."

Crank shuddered at the thought of anyone ever thinking Gore was nice. The last time the friends had seen him he was fighting off a band of robot pirates. Crank remembered hearing Gore roaring with anger — a sound that had carried through the night air and across the Ghost Sea like the cry of a wild animal — and seeing the glow from his flashing electro-blade as he destroyed any robot that dared to get in his way.

"Gore even saved my life once," continued Avatar. "He stepped in the way of a trap the Crodilus had set. I would have been crushed instantly but Gore is incredibly strong and came away with hardly a scratch."

"So what changed him?" asked Archimender.

"Gore was obsessed with space travel," said Avatar, "and he was determined to get enough credits to buy a craft of his own. Then it was discovered that he'd been selling things to the Crodilus."

"What sort of fings?" asked Grunt.

"Nothing much," said Avatar. "Just odd bits of technology that had been left lying around from when the softies were here, but it was enough to get Gore into trouble with the robot council."

"I am surprised they didn't have him destroyed," said Archimender.

"They would have done," agreed Avatar. "But he'd been a good member of the defence force, so instead Gore was banished from Tarka and told never to return. Of course, Gore wasn't happy about this and he vowed to have revenge – but no one saw him again and everyone presumed he must have been destroyed."

"Yeah, but it's like Gore said," nodded Grunt. "It's not dat easy to destroy him."

"You're right," said Avatar, and she told Archimender all about meeting Gore and the robot pirates of the Ghost Sea.

"I do not like the sound of this Gore," said Archimender.

"Don't worry about him," said Avatar. "I'm sure there will be nothing left of him by now – those robot pirates were quite vicious. Anyway, it looks like the city has enough trouble with the Crodilus without worrying about anything else."

Archimender agreed and led the three friends through the rest of the tunnel and into the hangar.

"Luckily, the hangar was one of the first buildings to be sealed with the new aqua-shell," said Archimender, showing them round. "Otherwise we wouldn't have had anything left to defend ourselves against the Crodilus."

Other than Archimender and the five Aquanauts that had brought them below the surface, the three friends hadn't seen anyone else since arriving in Aqua. No one had passed them in the tube they'd walked along and Crank hadn't spotted anyone in any of the other tubes either. He'd begun to think Aqua was deserted, but here in the hangar there were robots of all shapes and sizes.

Dragonflies and other vehicles that Crank didn't recognise were parked along the outsides of the room and computer equipment and assorted weapons took up every table and workspace.

Some of the robots were working on the craft while others were busy testing weapons or sitting at computer screens.

"They all look very busy," said Crank. "Is it always like this?"

"Not at all," said Archimender. "The robots are preparing for war."

"War!" said Crank. "But Aqua looks so peaceful."

"It was for a while," said Archimender, "but the Crodilus are coming and this time they will not leave until every last robot has been defeated."

"I said the Crodilus hated robots," said Avatar.

"You are wrong," said Archimender, leading the friends out of the hangar and into another of the long blue tubes. "The Crodilus do not *hate* robots. It is their love of technology and their desire to make themselves stronger that makes them fight us."

"Dat don't make no sense," said Grunt, scratching his head.

"The Crodilus have been replacing *their own* body-parts with *robotic* parts," explained Archimender. "The greatest Crodilus warriors are now more robot than Crodilus. They call themselves the Cro."

"Dat's disgusting," scowled Grunt. "We has met cyborgs before an' dey is not nice."

"You are right," said Archimender, "but you shouldn't worry about the Cro – this isn't your war and your friend is waiting for you. When you are ready I can show you a safe way out of the city."

"We thought Al had been destroyed," said Avatar. "One of the Crodilus attacked us in a Dragonfly."

"Yeah!" agreed Grunt. "It crashed into da walkway and Al fell into da water."

"Well he must have pulled himself out of the water," said Archimender. "We found him on the wall. It looked as though he had been in quite a battle but we have managed to repair him as best we can."

"I don't know how we can thank you," said Crank.

"Just being able to help another robot is thanks enough," said Archimender, leading the three friends into another small building.

As they entered the building the lights flickered for a moment and Archimender stood still and looked around.

"Oh dear!" he said. "I fear something is about to—"

Then the lights went off and everything went dark.

In the distance the friends could hear the dull rumbling of emergency generators powering up and the lamps on the wall started to glow faintly, shedding a dim light over everything.

"What is it?" asked Avatar.

"It could be nothing," said Archimender. "Or it could be—"

But Archimender didn't get to finish. In the distance an alarm had started wailing and the sound of distant explosions could be heard.

"It's the Cro," said Archimender. "They're here."

7

As Archimender rushed back along the tube
towards the hangar, Avatar went after him.

"Wait!" she cried. "We can help you."

"No!" said Archimender, stopping for a
moment. "Your future lies somewhere else. Now
go … your friends are waiting for you."

Avatar reluctantly turned round and headed
back along the tube and into the building where
the others were still waiting. Perhaps Archimender
was right, she thought. Perhaps her future *did* lie
somewhere else. After all, *Tarka* had been her city –
not this undersea hideaway – but she still couldn't
help feeling guilty about not going to help the

other robots in their fight against the Cro.

"Are you all right?" asked Crank, as Avatar joined them again.

"Yes," she replied. "But I keep thinking that things would have been different if I'd stayed in Tarka all those years ago, instead of travelling round in search of Robotika."

"Yeah," agreed Grunt. "It *would* be different. You would have bin destroyed wiv all da other robots when da city flooded."

"He's right," said Crank. "And *this* time you *will* find Robotika because you won't be on your own. You'll be with us ... your friends."

Avatar smiled and nodded at Crank and Grunt. "You're right," she said. "And Al's waiting here for us too, isn't he?"

There were a few doors leading off the darkened hallway where they stood and Al could have been behind any of them, but Scamp was standing patiently by one of the doors, wagging his tail.

"Has you found 'im, Scamp?" asked Grunt, patting the robo-dog on the head with one huge hand. "Good boy."

Avatar put her hand on the door handle and was about to open it when Crank stopped her.

"You do think he'll be all right, don't you?" he said. "Archimender said it looked as though he'd been in a battle."

"Archimender also said they'd fixed him up as well as they could," said Avatar reassuringly.

"It's just that Al's such a new robot," said Crank, looking worried. "He should never even have left Metrocity in the first place. It's all my fault that he ended up going to the recycling plant and getting his legs pulled off."

"Don't you worry," said Grunt. "Dat Al is quite a tough little guy really."

"But if he's all right then why hasn't he come out here to see us?" said Crank. "He must have heard us talking."

"These doors are quite thick," said Avatar, "*and* they have to be opened from the outside. So why don't we just open it and then we can see for ourselves."

"Of course," said Crank, grabbing the handle. "I'm sorry. Here ... let me do it."

Crank pulled on the handle and, with a clunk, the heavy door swung slowly open.

It was dark inside the room and the three friends could hardly see a thing. The light from the hallway barely even touched the darkness.

"Nah!" said Grunt, shaking his head. "Looks empty to me. Let's try one of de others."

"You're not afraid of the dark, are you, Grunt?" asked Avatar.

"Course not," said Grunt, sounding a little embarrassed. "I just likes to be able to see fings, dat's all."

"Well I think I can see him," said Avatar, stepping into the room. "I'm sure there's a robot on that bed over there. It looks like Al's been having a recharge. There's power wires all over the place."

Crank stumbled into the room behind Avatar and tripped over a power cable that was stretched across the floor.

"Aarghhh!" he yelled, falling to the floor and pulling the power cable out of the wall. Something heavy slid across a nearby table and Crank just managed to roll out of the way as a small generator crashed to the floor beside him.

"When you have quite finished," whispered Avatar, "I am sure this is not the best way to reactivate Al after all he's been through."

"All *he's* been through?" said Crank. "What about me?"

Crank was about to say more but as he got to his feet he noticed the dark shape on the bed was beginning to move. The robot was getting up.

"Oh! Hello, Al," said Crank. "Sorry about all the noise but we're so pleased to see you again. We thought you'd been … er …"

"Yeah," interrupted Grunt. "We fought you'd been … er … y'know …"

"Recycled? Crushed?" suggested the robot. "You should know me better than that. No one *ever* gets Gore – Gore gets them."

"What did 'e say?" said Grunt.

Two eyes suddenly lit up in the robot's face – one red and one yellow, burning in the darkness of the room.

"Al? What's happened to your eyes?" said Crank. "They look—"

"GET BACK!" yelled Avatar.

But it was too late.

Before Crank realised what was happening, a

huge metal fist hit him in the face and sent him flying backwards across the room. As Crank crashed into a row of shelves, the big robot leaped off the bed and dashed towards the door. Crank was just able to see it silhouetted in the doorway before the shelves collapsed on top of him, covering him with tools and spare robot parts.

Even though he'd only managed to get a quick glimpse of the robot, Crank knew who it was.

He'd recognised the row of spikes that ran along the centre of its head and on its huge shoulders. As the robot had disappeared through the doorway he'd also seen the clawed hand, and Crank only knew one robot with a hand like that.

"Oo!" said Grunt, shaking his head. "Somefink tells me dat Al isn't in a good mood."

"That wasn't Al," said Avatar, helping Crank get out from beneath the pile of tools and spare parts. "That was Gore."

"WHAT!" roared Grunt. "I fought 'e was gone for good."

"Well it looks like we were wrong," said Avatar.

"Come on ... we'll have to stop him."

"But what about Al?" asked Crank.

"I don't think Al was ever here," said Avatar. "It was Gore they found. That explains why they found him on the wall and not in the water like we'd expected. Gore must been following us from the Ghost Sea."

"Me an' Scamp knew *somefink* was following us," said Grunt. "But I didn't know what it was ... hey ... where *is* Scamp?"

As he spoke, the three friends heard a loud metallic howl come echoing from outside the room.

"SCAMP!" cried Grunt, charging past his two friends to the connection tube that led back towards the hangar.

When they found him, Scamp was lying on his side in the middle of the tube with one leg twisted behind him.

"Dat Gore will be sorry," said Grunt. "No one hurts poor little Scamp and gets away wiv it."

The thought of anyone being strong enough to be able to hurt the big robo-dog made Crank's circuits shake with fear. He'd already seen what the botweiler could do to other robots and this showed just how powerful Gore really was.

"Come on," said Avatar. "We've got to stop him before he does any more damage."

"I is not leaving Scamp here," said Grunt,

picking the robo-dog up in his arms.

As they ran along the tube towards the hangar, Crank noticed something going on beneath the water outside and stopped for a closer look. Last time they'd gone along the tube everything had looked peaceful and Crank had seen fish swimming between the ruins of the flooded city.

There was no sign of any fish now, but instead, three Aquanauts were lumbering past the outside of the tube with huge energy guns in their hands. In the distance, Crank could see what looked like a giant manta ray swimming towards them ... but something didn't look quite right.

Crank watched the manta ray for a few seconds trying to work out what was wrong with it. It wasn't moving like the ray he'd seen earlier, gliding gracefully through the water; this one seemed more mechanical.

It wasn't until the manta ray got closer that Crank saw the Crodilus sitting on its back. As he

watched,
balls of green fire
shot from the front of the
manta ray as the Crodilus fired
its twin plasma cannons at the Aquanauts.

Crank banged on the side of the tube wall,
trying to warn the Aquanauts, but it was no use …
they couldn't hear him.

The first two plasma balls hit the ground in front
of them, throwing up clouds of dirt and frightening
a large eel that had been hiding in the mud.

As the Aquanauts slowly turned round to see what was happening, the second two plasma balls reached them. One whizzed harmlessly past but the other was right on target and the green ball hit one of the Aquanauts in the chest, knocking it off its feet and throwing it against the outside of the tube wall.

The Aquanaut fell to the floor, dropping its energy gun, and the robot inside was struggling to get back up when the Manta Ray fired again. Two more balls of green plasma hissed through the water, one hitting the Aquanaut and the other exploding against the wall of the tube in front of Crank's face.

A long crack appeared in the tube wall where the plasma ball had exploded, and outside Crank saw the Aquanaut staggering around for a few moments, streams of tiny bubbles escaping from all the joints in its armour as it filled with water.

The two remaining Aquanauts lifted their energy

guns and fired back at the Manta Ray. Bolts of raw energy shot through the water, some flying past but others exploding as they hit the Manta Ray.

The Manta Ray twisted and turned through the water, trying to dodge the energy bolts and fire back with its plasma cannons at the same time. As it turned, one of the energy bolts hit the Crodilus pilot, knocking it from its seat and leaving the craft to continue through the water on its own.

Crank watched as the two Aquanauts quickly started to rise up towards the surface, away from the Manta Ray, then realised the craft was heading straight towards the tube where he was standing.

Water was already seeping in through the crack in the tube wall and if the Manta Ray hit it …

"RUN!" yelled Crank, setting off along the tube as fast as he could.

Grunt and Avatar were a long way ahead when Crank caught up with them but there was still a little way to go before they reached the hangar.

"Faster," yelled Crank. "The tube's going to flood!"

"Nah!" said Grunt, walking along with Scamp in his arms. "Dese tubes is very strong. Dis aqua-shell is pretty tough stuff."

"But there's going to be a cra—"

The crash shook the whole tube and a loud roaring sound could be heard coming from behind them.

Grunt slowed down to look back over his shoulder then suddenly sped up as he saw the first splashes of water coming round the bend towards them.

"WATER!" yelled Grunt, and charged past Crank, with Scamp still held tightly in his arms.

As the three friends ran they could hear the roar of the water as it flooded into the broken tube. It hurtled round the twists and turns at a frightening speed, crashing into the walls and threatening to engulf the robots at any second.

Avatar reached the end of the tunnel first and had the door into the hangar open by the time Grunt and Crank reached it.

"Come on," she shouted as the two robots sped towards her.

Once they were through, Avatar started to push the heavy door closed, but water was already starting to flood through it.

"Help!" she cried, as the water sprayed round the edges of the door. "We've got to get this door closed."

Crank joined Avatar leaning against the door but it wasn't until Grunt joined in and put his shoulder against it that the three friends managed to push the heavy door closed against the force of the raging water.

Being so busy with the door, the friends hadn't even noticed what had been going on in the hangar behind them. Scamp had been lying on the floor where Grunt had laid him and it wasn't until the robo-dog let out a loud growl that the others turned round.

"Good boy, Scamp," said Grunt, seeing the botweiler get up and limp across the floor. "I knew he'd be back on 'is feet soon."

Then they saw what the big botweiler was growling at.

Crank hadn't really had a chance to take a good look at one of the Crodilus before. He'd only caught a glimpse of their long mouths, sharp teeth and scaly bodies. He thought that had been bad enough, but standing in front of them now, with a robot gripped in its hand, was a creature even more terrible than he'd imagined.

The creature reminded Crank of the old vid-films he'd seen about crocodiles – huge lizard-like creatures that had crawled on their bellies through the swamps and rivers of the planet many years ago. But instead of crawling, the Crodilus stood upright on muscular legs and wore armour over parts of its body and along its tail.

One of its arms was entirely metal, taken from some unfortunate robot, and it only had one yellow eye in its hideous head. The other had been replaced with a robotic eye that glowed bright red so it reminded Crank of Gore.

The Cro grinned, baring its teeth, and dropped the robot it had been holding. As the robot clattered to the floor its head flopped to one side so it was facing the three friends.

Crank recognised the robot instantly. It was Archimender.

With a growl, Scamp leaped through the air, his teeth bared in a ferocious snarl and his razor-sharp claws out, ready to shred and tear.

Crank knew how deadly the robo-dog's teeth and claws could be, but the Crodilus hardly even flinched as the big robo-dog flew through the air towards it. Instead, it casually knocked Scamp away with the back of one hand as if it had been swatting a fly.

With a whine, the robo-dog clattered to the ground and crashed into one of the upturned tables that now littered the floor of the hangar.

Seeing what had happened to Scamp, Grunt

charged towards the Cro, pulling one huge fist back, ready to knock it through the wall. But the Cro quickly stepped to one side and held out its arm, catching Grunt beneath his chin.

As Grunt landed flat on his back with a heavy crunch, Avatar gracefully somersaulted through the air, kicked the Cro in the chest with one foot and sent it staggering backwards.

Avatar didn't wait for the Cro to recover but stepped forwards and punched it on the chin with one hand then in the chest with the other.

"How do you like that, you big lizard?" said Avatar, ducking out of the way as the Cro lunged towards her.

Letting out an angry roar, the Cro jumped towards her again and this time Avatar leaped backwards and bumped straight into Crank.

There was a crash as the two robots fell to the floor and the Cro let out a howling laugh.

"So disappointing," it hissed. "I thought you

would have put up more of a fight than that."

Crank and Avatar were picking themselves up off the floor when they heard the hiss and click of an energy gun powering up.

"Such a waste of good parts," hissed the Cro, pointing the energy gun at the two friends, "but I haven't got time to play around any more."

Crank closed his eyes and waited for the bolt of energy to hit him, but instead there was just a soft thud.

Opening his eyes again, Crank saw that the Cro seemed to have frozen for a moment as if it was wondering what to do. Then the energy gun dropped from its hands, clattered to the floor, and the creature fell to its knees before finally falling face down on to the ground in front of them.

Stood behind the unconscious Cro, Archimender was examining the metal bar in his hand.

"You can't mess around with those creatures," he said, throwing the metal bar away. "A good whack on the head normally sorts them out."

"We thought you'd been destroyed," said Avatar, happy to see that Archimender was still well.

"Oh no," said the old robot, shaking his head.

"It will take more than a big lizard to finish me off."

Grunt was just getting to his feet as Scamp limped over to him with his head and tail hanging down. "It's all right," said Grunt, patting the robo-dog's head with one huge hand. "Dat Cro was quite a handful. It even knocked old Grunt off 'is feet."

"Yes," agreed Archimender. "They are terrible creatures and we haven't seen the last of them yet."

"You mean there's more?" said Crank, looking around nervously.

"Oh yes," said Archimender. "Lots more, and I am afraid we may be the last of the robots."

"What about the others?" said Avatar.

"The Cro have taken them," said Archimender, sadly. "Now you should leave before any of them return."

"But what about you?" said Crank. "You can come with us."

"No, no, no," said Archimender, shaking his head. "I am much too old to leave the city."

"You can't just stay here," said Avatar. "The Cro will come for you too."

"Don't worry," said Archimender. "I can escape if there's an emergency. Now come on," continued the old robot. "You will have to leave using one of the aqua-spheres."

Archimender led the three friends back to the little building where they had first entered the underwater city. Inside, Crank noticed that the Aquanaut pods were empty and he wondered whether any of the Aquanauts he'd seen earlier were still all right.

"Here it is," said Archimender, laying a box on the floor in front of the robots, "the very last sphere. I kept it hidden in case of an emergency."

"Well, this is an emergency," said Avatar. "So you should get in the sphere and come with us."

"We can't all get in," said Archimender. "One of us needs to activate the sphere."

The three friends stood together with Scamp between them while Archimender placed the box on the floor in front of them.

"But this was *your* emergency escape route," said Crank. "You've got to come with us."

"Don't forget," said Archimender, "I've got my own Aquanaut suit."

Archimender smiled at the friends and activated the aqua-sphere, then stepped back out of the way as the box bleeped three times. A pool of bright blue gel seeped out from the box and poured across the floor.

The gel fizzed and crackled as it crept beneath the robots' feet then started to rise into the air to form a giant sphere around them.

Crank reached out and gently touched the wall of the sphere as it formed around them, then realised what he'd seen before.

"There *are* no Aquanaut suits," he cried. "They've all been taken."

Archimender just smiled. "It seems that your friend took it," he said. "But that doesn't matter. This city is my home. I could never leave it."

"Our friend?" said Avatar, wondering who the old robot was talking about.

Then she realised.

"Gore!" she cried. "I'd forgotten about him. Gore has taken the last Aquanaut suit."

Avatar banged on the wall of the sphere and waved her arms around.

"It wasn't our friend," shouted Avatar. "That was Gore."

But the sphere had completely sealed around the three friends and the old robot could no longer hear them.

Archimender waved goodbye and stepped out of the room, leaving the robots sealed in the pale blue sphere. Once the door had closed behind him they heard the hum of giant pumps and the room started to fill with water.

10

There was nothing the three friends could do but
wait as the water level in the room began to rise.
When it was completely full the roof of the
building opened and, without anything to hold it
down, the sphere slowly floated up to the surface
of the water where it bobbed about in the sunlight.

"It's good to be out of the water," said Crank,
peering through pale blue surface of the aqua-
sphere.

"We isn't out of it yet," said Grunt. "We've still
got to get out of dis fing."

"We'll have to be careful as well," said Avatar.
"Gore could be out here somewhere."

"He could be anywhere," said Crank. "What are we going to do?"

"Archimender said we should head for the old library tower," said Avatar. "It's over there."

"I meant what are we going to do about Gore?" said Crank.

"This isn't the time to worry about him," said Avatar. "Now come on."

The three friends found they could move the sphere across the water in the direction they wanted by simply walking. It wasn't easy at first but they soon got the hang of it and had the giant ball rolling through the water towards the library tower.

Luckily there weren't too many obstacles in their way, though they did have to steer between the pillars of a couple of walkways. Through the cloudy blue surface of the sphere it was difficult to see just how far they had to go and they were surprised when the sphere suddenly hit something.

The sphere jolted and bounced as it rolled out
of the water and on to a landing platform. Crank
fell forwards, hitting his face with a loud crack.
Grunt landed on top of him and Avatar tripped
over them both.

"I think we're here," said Avatar, picking herself
up. "This looks like the library tower right in front
of us now."

"Great," said Crank. "Now *how* are we going
to get out of here? Last time they used an energy

gun to break the aqua-sphere."

"Don't worry," said Grunt, clenching one hand. "Openin' fings is my speciality."

Grunt had clenched his fist and pulled his arm back, ready to punch the wall of the sphere, when there was a sudden bang.

The aqua-sphere around them exploded, showering the robots in sticky blue gel.

"I must be good," said Grunt. "I never even touched it."

As the robots wiped the gel from their faces there was an explosion on the platform next to them as an energy bolt hit it.

"Someone is firing at us," said Avatar, as she set off running across the platform towards an arched doorway at the bottom of the library tower.

"It's one of dem Aquanauts," said Grunt. "Why is dey firing at us?"

"That's not an Aquanaut," said Crank. "That's Gore. Archimender said he'd taken his suit."

A third energy bolt exploded on the stones around the doorway and a fourth skimmed past the side of Crank's head as he disappeared through it and into the safety of the tower.

"That was close," said Crank, trying to examine the side of his head.

"Come on," said Avatar, running up the steps. "We can get across to the north wall from the top of this tower."

"Yeah," said Grunt. "Come on. We hasn't got time to stand around lookin' at our ears. Unless you wants Gore to come an' pull dem off for you."

Crank ran up the steps two at a time and was at the top only a few steps behind the others.

"There's no sign of Gore," said Crank, looking behind them.

"It will take him ages to get across here in dat big Aquanaut suit," said Grunt.

Avatar agreed and was about to open the door at the top of the tower when Crank stopped her.

"What is it?" she asked.

"This door will lead us out of the city," said Crank, "and it just doesn't seem right to be leaving without Al."

"I know," said Avatar, nodding her head sadly, "but I'm sure he would have wanted us to carry on even if he wasn't here."

"You're right," said Crank. "I suppose we should go."

Avatar pushed the door open and the robots stepped out and on to the narrow walkway beyond it – the walkway that bridged the last stretch of water and would take them away from the ancient city. The friends took a few steps and then froze.

Standing facing them in the middle of the walkway was one of the huge Aquanauts.

"It's him," said Crank, hardly daring to move. "It's Gore."

"It can't be," said Avatar.

"But it is," said Crank. "He's wearing

Archimender's suit."

"But—" said Grunt.

"It's got the lightning stripes," said Crank.

"Archimender's was the only suit that had those."

"Why is 'e not movin' den?" said Grunt.

Avatar slowly walked towards the huge

Aquanaut, expecting it to attack at any moment –

but it didn't. It just stood there, motionless.

She carefully reached out and touched the Aquanaut's arm, but still it didn't move. "Gore?" said Avatar. "Are you all right?"

As soon as she touched it, the huge Aquanaut tipped sideways and fell off the narrow walkway, spinning through the air until it splashed into the water far below.

"Well," said Grunt, "dat was easy. Perhaps Gore wasn't as tough as you fought?"

"Gore wasn't in there," said Avatar. "That Aquanaut suit was empty."

"So what's happened to Gore?" asked Crank.

From behind them came the unmistakable hiss and click of an energy gun powering up. The three friends turned to see Gore standing there with his back to the tower door.

"Those Aquanaut 3000 suits are very good," said Gore. "And so much quicker than walking."

"But we fought you was—"

"Gone?" suggested Gore. "You didn't think it would be that easy, did you? You should know by now, no one gets rid of Gore ... Gore gets rid of them."

Then the door behind him burst open, and with a loud cry the big robot was knocked off the narrow walkway.

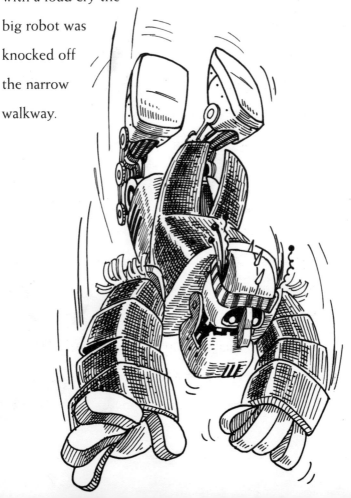

The three friends watched as Gore fell through the air and landed with a heavy crunch on the platform at the bottom of the tower.

"Oh dear!" said Al, looking down at the mess of robot parts far below.

"I hope I did not hurt anyone."

"AL!" cried the three friends.

"Sorry it has taken me so long to catch up with

you all," said Al, "but it was quite difficult finding a place to get out of the water."

"But, but, but," said Crank.

"Yes?" said Al, looking puzzled.

"We thought you—" said Crank.

"Yeah!" agreed Grunt. We fought you'd been—"

"Destroyed? Crushed?" suggested Al, as the others set off across the narrow walkway. "You should know that it is not *that* easy to get rid of me. You must have forgotten I am the very latest in robot technology and I am constructed from—

"HEY! Wait for me," shouted Al, running to catch up with the others. "Where are you going?"

"We're off to find a safe place for old robots," said Crank.

"Yeah," said Grunt. "A place where robots can be free to live dare lives in peace."

"A place called Robotika," said Avatar.

*

Leaving the ancient flooded city behind them, four robot friends set off across the North Polar Wastelands with a big robo-dog beside them.

"Do you think we will ever find Robotika?" asked Al, switching off his anti-grav belt so he could walk for a while.

"Of course we will," said Crank.

In the distance the lights of the North Polar Spaceport flickered in the evening sky.

"Perhaps someone over dare can help us," suggested Grunt.

"We'll see," said Avatar. "We'll see."

The End

CRANK

AL

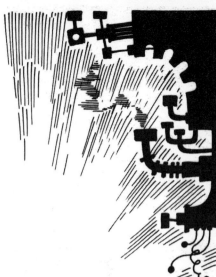

AVATAR

GRUNT

book 1

The Tin man

The giant metal claw hanging above the bath had swung round and grabbed Crank round the waist. Crank used all his strength to try and get free from the claw's steely grip … but it was no use. He found himself being carried up and over the side of the bath.

Crank just had time for a final look at his friends. He could hardly believe his eyes. The other robots were sitting there as if nothing was happening. Even Al didn't seem concerned. *Some friends*, he thought, as the claw started to lower him towards the liquid.

Bubbles erupted fiercely below him and clouds of foul-smelling gas rose into the air. Crank was sure the bath was full of acid and he was about to be dissolved.

"Arghhhhhh!" he screamed, as the steel claw lowered him into the bath, "I'm melting …"

DAMIAN HARVEY

lives in Blackpool with his wife and three daughters, their four cats, a horde of guinea pigs, a tank full of fish and a quirky imagination.

He loves music, movies, reading, swimming, walking, cheese and ice cream – but not always at the same time.

Before realising how much fun he could have writing and making things up he worked as a lifeguard, had a job in a boring office and once saved the galaxy from invading vampire robots (though none of these were as exciting as they sound).

Damian now spends lots of time in front of his computer but loves getting out to visit schools and libraries to share stories, talk about writing and get people excited about books.